PRAISE FOR M. L. BUCHMAN

Top 10 Romance of 2012, 2015, and 2016.

— BOOKLIST: THE NIGHT IS MINE, HOT POINT,
HEART STRIKE

One of our favorite authors.

— RT BOOK REVIEWS

Buchman has catapulted his way to the top tier of my favorite authors.

— FRESH FICTION

A favorite author of mine. I'll read anything that carries his name, no questions asked. Meet your new favorite author!

— THE SASSY BOOKSTER, FLASH OF FIRE

M.L. Buchman is guaranteed to get me lost in a good story.

— THE READING CAFE, WAY OF THE WARRIOR:
NSDQ

I love Buchman's writing. His vivid descriptions bring everything to life in an unforgettable way.

— PURE JONEL, HOT POINT

WELCOME AT HENDERSON'S RANCH

A HENDERSON'S RANCH ROMANCE STORY

M. L. BUCHMAN

Buchman Bookworks

SIGN UP FOR M. L. BUCHMAN'S
NEWSLETTER TODAY

and receive:
Release News
Free Short Stories
a Free Starter Library

Do it today. Do it now.
www.mlbuchman.com/newsletter

Other works by M. L. Buchman:

The Night Stalkers

MAIN FLIGHT

The Night Is Mine
I Own the Dawn
Wait Until Dark
Take Over at Midnight
Light Up the Night
Bring On the Dusk
By Break of Day

WHITE HOUSE HOLIDAY

Daniel's Christmas
Frank's Independence Day
Peter's Christmas
Zachary's Christmas
Roy's Independence Day
Damien's Christmas

AND THE NAVY

Christmas at Steel Beach
Christmas at Peleliu Cove

5E

Target of the Heart
Target Lock on Love
Target of Mine

Firehawks

MAIN FLIGHT

Pure Heat
Full Blaze
Hot Point
Flash of Fire
Wild Fire

SMOKEJUMPERS

Wildfire at Dawn
Wildfire at Larch Creek
Wildfire on the Skagit

Delta Force

Target Engaged
Heart Strike
Wild Justice

Where Dreams

Where Dreams are Born
Where Dreams Reside
Where Dreams Are of Christmas
Where Dreams Unfold
Where Dreams Are Written

Eagle Cove

Return to Eagle Cove
Recipe for Eagle Cove
Longing for Eagle Cove
Keepsake for Eagle Cove

Henderson's Ranch

Nathan's Big Sky

Love Abroad

Heart of the Cotswolds: England

Dead Chef Thrillers

Swap Out!
One Chef!
Two Chef!

Deities Anonymous

Cookbook from Hell: Reheated
Saviors 101

SF/F Titles

The Nara Reaction
Monk's Maze
the Me and Elsie Chronicles

Strategies for Success (NF)

Managing Your Inner Artist/Writer
Estate Planning for Authors

Dateline: August 15, Henderson's Ranch,
   Bloody Nowhere, Montana

Colleen McMurphy could write this article in her sleep, with her keyboard tied behind her back, and…

"The wife and I had such a splendid time there. You simply must go and write us an article about it." For some reason Larry always went old-school English whenever he got excited—which coming from her Puerto Rican boss who lived in Seattle seemed to be almost normal for Colleen's life.

He, of course, was too busy being Mr. Hotshot Editor to write it himself. That and he couldn't write his way out of a martini glass. He was one of the best editors she'd ever worked for—and as a freelancer that had included a suckload of them—but his twelve-year-old daughter could write new material better than he could. Hillary was named for Sir Edmund of Mt. Everest fame and just might follow her namesake at the rate she was being amazing. She was a precocious little twerp who was so delightful that she made

Colleen feel grossly inadequate half the time and totally charmed the other three-quarters.

So, off to Montana it was. Magazine feature article—she was on it.

The most recent in a cascade of ever-shrinking planes banged onto the runway in Great Falls, Montana clicking all Colleen's vertebrae together with a whip-like snap that surprisingly failed to paralyze her. A Japan Airlines 747 had lofted her from the family home in Tokyo to LAX. The smallest 737 ever made hopped her up to Salt Lake, and a wing-flapping 18-seater express fluttered as hopelessly as a just-fledged swallow to Great Falls. If there'd been another plane that was any smaller, they were going to have to put her in a bento box.

But finally she was here in…major sigh…Nowhere, Montana.

She'd used this job as an excuse to cut the two-week trip home in half. Two weeks! *With her family?* What *had* she been thinking? She was going to have a serious talk with her sense of filial duty before it dragged her from Seattle back to Japan again.

Outside the miniature plane's windows the airport stretched away pancake-flat and dusty. Four whole jetways, the place was *smaller* than a bento box. But their plane didn't pull up to any of them—because it was too short to reach. Instead, it stopped near the terminal and the copilot dropped the door open, filling the cabin with the familiar bite of spent engine fumes and slowing propeller roar. She'd spent the whole final flight glaring out at the spinning blades directly outside her window, waiting for one to break off, punch through the window, and slice her in two like one of Larry's martini olives.

"Enough!" she told herself so loudly that it made the fatboy businessman—who'd made the near-fatal mistake of trying to chat her up across the tiny aisle—jump in alarm. Twenty hours and nine minutes in flight didn't usually make her this grouchy. Her parents did though.

"Why did you change your name?" *Because everyone in America would laugh their faces off calling her Kurva—for the Hokkaido mulberry tree you conceived me under, much too much information by the way. It especially doesn't translate so well for a girl who is Japanese flat. Besides there isn't an American alive who can say* Baisotei *properly.* Kurva Baisotei was not a money-making byline.

Then, not "When are you going to get married?" but rather "Why do you not give us grandchildren like your sister?" *My sister has three. How insatiable are you as grandparents?*

"Why do you not return home?" *Because you live here.*

"Ma'am?" Fat-boy was waiting for her to get out of her seat first. Maybe because he needed the full width of the tiny plane, or maybe he was just being nice. She was about to step back on American soil—even if it was Montana—so she gave him the benefit of the doubt and offered a "Thanks" with a smile that hopefully he didn't read as encouraging.

The air outside the airport smelled strange. It definitely wasn't Seattle, which had an evergreen scent that wrapped itself around you like a warm, though often damp, welcome home. Her best girl Ruth Ann always met her when she landed from trips to Japan to drag her to their favorite dive, the J&M in Pioneer Square, and make sure that she got safely drunk within an hour of landing. It was doubly strange to arrive somewhere else without Ruth Ann's patiently sympathetic ear.

Montana was dry and, despite the warm afternoon, somehow crisp. In Seattle there were a gazillion things sharing the air with her: Douglas firs, seagulls, dogs playing in the park, ferry boats—the list went on and on. Here it tasted more rarified. More…special.

Also high on the *special* list was the guy leaning comfortably on a helicopter with "Henderson's Ranch" emblazoned down the side like it had been branded there with a flaming iron. He already had one beaming couple beside him with Los Angeles cowboy written all over their Gucci. He towered above them: six-two of dark tan, right-out-of-a-romance-novel square jaw, and mirrored shades for a touch of mystery. His t-shirt was tight and his jeans weren't bad either. And—crap!—ring on his finger. Fantasy cowboys weren't supposed to have rings on their fingers, but she wasn't going to complain about this piece of the Montana scenery just because of the "Back Off" sign.

Another couple joined them. First-timers by their lost look.

"Hi!" He even had a nice deep voice to go with that big frame. "I'm Mark Henderson. Climb on aboard," and he was helping the two couples into the back seats.

Handsome guy who flies a helicopter. Sweet! Maybe Montana wasn't going to be so bad. Ruth Ann was gonna be wicked jealous. She snapped a photo of him just for that purpose.

"Looks like you're up front with me, beautiful," he aimed a lethal smile directly at her.

She returned the smile, feeling pleased. Then lost it when she realized the implications.

Two happy couples in the back.

Handsome married dude in the front.

And that's when the background research she'd done on their website finally made a horrible kind of sense. Weddings this. Couples that. Family horseback rides the other. Larry should have sent Colleen's perfect sister's family, not her.

She was a single Japanese chick, with an Irish name she'd

taken from the old TV show *China Beach*. (She'd always liked the main character—strong woman back when that wasn't a very popular thing to be.)

Be strong now!

She was going to a couples' paradise. This was going to be worse than the parental purgatory.

She'd be pleasant. Polite.

And as soon as she got home, Larry was a dead man.

2

Montana greets visitors who fly in with the dullest landscape imaginable. Rulers are tested here for an accurate straight edge by laying them on the ground.

But fifty miles to the west, the Rocky Mountains soar aloft, forcing the eye to constantly scan upward to the bluest sky imaginable. Henderson's Ranch lies nestled in the softly rolling country at the base of these majestic peaks.

A night's sleep and Colleen felt much more human this morning, even if she couldn't make sense of what lay outside her cabin window. To the south and east, the land stretched so far away that she felt as if she was perched atop an infinite cliff and at the least misstep might tumble down forever. A person could get vertigo here just sitting still.

To the west, the mountains punched aloft in bold, jagged

strokes with little of the softness that Washington's forests provided to Seattle's peaks.

There was a wildness that confronted her every time she looked at these mountains. Her inner city Tokyo childhood, her rebellious escape to the community of fifty-thousand students at the University of Washington, Seattle's million people—none of it prepared her for this stark emptiness.

Here along the Front Range, aside from a few dozen guests and another dozen ranch hands, there might not be a soul for twenty miles. It felt like a thousand.

Down the slope, a tall woman stepped out of the back door of the main lodge and rang a giant steel triangle just like in an Old West movie: *clangety-clangety-clangety-clang.*

Families and couples streamed out of the other cabins and headed downhill toward the massive two-story log cabin structure that looked like one of those Depression-era lodges. Huge, powerful, unmoving.

A quick survey showed that she was the only singleton— if she didn't count kids, and even they seemed to come in packs. Almost everyone was dressed in K-Mart Western, or some designer version that looked no more likely.

There were breakfast fixings in her cabin, and she was tempted to retreat there, but she was here to write a travelogue article. For that she had to experience the experience.

She was last down the trail to the big house. The guests were all guided along the wrap-around porch to the front entrance into the big dining room she'd seen on last night's welcome tour. Thirty people could eat communal style at the long table.

However, a few others were coming around to the kitchen door. They were dressed far more casually, and far more authentically. Cowboy boots, dusty jeans, a variety of hats—some battered cowboy, some baseball-cap redneck. The women were dressed much the same.

Not really paying attention to what her feet were doing, she fell in with the ranch hands and found herself in a massive and beautiful kitchen. The hands were making use of one of the sinks before gathering at a smaller version of the big communal table out front.

"Mornin', Colleen. Not up for our 'Happy Couples' breakfast?" Mark the pilot greeted her with an understanding smile, reading her too easily.

Time to gear up the pleasant-reporter face.

He wasn't any less handsome this morning, but a stunning blonde kissed him on the cheek as she topped up his coffee, confirming that the ring wasn't just for show.

"Not so much, if that's okay."

"Take a seat. Dad's this one, Mom's the other end, when she bothers to sit down. The rest are up for grabs."

She took a seat almost, but not quite, at the middle of the table on the far side. It gave her the best view of what was going on and would let her hear most of the conversations without being the center of them. No one so much as blinked an eye as she joined them. A pretty redhead gave her a South California, "Hey!" Her husband was more the quiet-nod type.

Another long blonde gave her a very authentic sounding, "Howdy!" just as the male cook (with a Brooklyn-tinged "Hello and welcome") came and set a plate in front of the blonde, then kissed her on top of the head.

Shit! She was in Couplandia here as well. Finally some more guys came in until there was a fair balance of single men. More what she'd expected.

Her goal of keeping track of the conversations went out the window in the first ten seconds. They were talking about the day to come and what they knew about the guests, but doing it in a handful of simultaneous discussions: "Most of this lot we won't get out of the corral for a couple days." "Did you see that absolute babe from England? Never saw a woman sit a horse so *purty*. She'll ride far and hard." His companion—alike enough to be his twin—gave him a knowing smile that was all about the woman and not so much about how she sat.

Colleen stayed focused on her meal and her article. The food was incredibly good despite how basic a hash brown-and-ham scramble with a biscuit buried in gravy sounded. Article ideas were perking up as she enjoyed the camaraderie around the table. These people liked each other. Liked working together. And whatever else they were saying about the guests, none of it was bitter or caustic. She'd expected some derision of "city cowboys" but nothing even remotely like that came up in any of the several threads she was able to follow.

She wondered what they'd be saying about *her* behind her back.

"I like the way you listen."

It took her a moment to rewind the comment because it was only the last word that actually caught her attention. She finally traced it (nearly accentless) to the man across the table. He wasn't a big man—Colleen had an absolute weak spot for big men, who thankfully often had a weak spot for petite Japanese women—but he had a nice smile so she wouldn't hold his normalness of height and build against him.

"Uh-huh," her cordial-meter was still running below normal, but then no one was supposed to see through her pleasant-reporter face. She really needed another mug of tea.

"Heard you just arrived from Japan. Family there?"

"Uh-huh," her cordial-meter bottomed out. That was a reminder that she didn't need.

"Apparently the wrong question."

"Uh-huh," she dialed up her emphatic-sarcasm mode to full.

"Do you ride?"

Her first temptation was to go to "uh-uh" but she already was being subverbal far beyond her norm. Besides, it was the easiest response. Like writing, the easiest word (the first word she thought of) was rarely the most precise or evocative one. Good writing required avoiding the obvious while still telling the story—whether it encapsulated what it was like to work on the Boeing manufacturing line like her last article or the current purgatory of Couplandia.

Her interlocuter (yes! her vocabulary was finally coming back online) looked like a nice enough guy. Cowboy lean with a pleasant smile. She supposed that she'd have to ride a horse to get the full "Henderson's Ranch" experience and a private lesson sounded far better than shaming herself in public.

"Not yet," she added a smile which she knew was one of her strengths. The guy returned with a powerful one of his own.

It was only then that she noticed Mr. Handsome-with-a-ring Henderson rolling his eyes at her—at least that's what she assumed he was doing behind his ever-present shades.

Okay, maybe she could have been a little more subtle. But he said he liked the way she listened—one of the skills she was most proud of. That bit of insightfulness was going to earn him a lot of leeway.

3

Dateline, Day Four—

Colleen turned on a light against the fading day and flipped back through her notes again. Where had Day Three gone? Where had Day Two gone for that matter?

She finally found Day Two.

Mac Henderson, technically Mark Henderson, Sr. and almost as handsome as his son, had been thrilled to have her on the ranch. Apparently she was their first journalist, so their resort had a lot riding on making her happy—though he acted as if he was simply glad *she* was here, not several million readers AAA magazine would be sending this out to. Which was sweet of him to pretend.

On Day Two, he'd toured her about: cabins, yurts, cooking classes, weaving classes, horseback riding, even a military dog trainer named Stan—a big, gruff man with a hook prosthetic on one arm who only spoke to his dogs.

As the day had progressed, Mac had grown more and more excited about showing her around his ranch until he was as wound up as one of Stan's puppies. A former Navy

SEAL in his sixties who almost wriggled with delight. She'd always thought SEALs were supposed to be broody and stoic, but Mac was a thoroughly pleasant guy who clearly loved this land with a passion.

What she'd found truly unbelievable was the amount of work it took to run the place, and Mac made sure that she had a chance to meet and chat with every person of the staff. The redhead who ran the barn was so voluble that Colleen couldn't have gotten down one word in ten no matter how fast she took notes—and she was fast. Her husband, the ranch manager, was laconic to the point where Colleen wondered if people catnapped between his sentences.

It took her a while to catch on that he was teasing her with it.

Day Two afternoon: Mark's wife Emily took her on a solo helicopter flight over the ranch that was stunning in both its expansiveness and its variety. The softly rolling landscape around the buildings gave way to rugged prairie, patches of pine forest, and even waterfalls along a small river that ran down out of the hills. A group of horses out at a remote fishing cabin revealed that at least some riders had made it past the corral.

The cook wasn't a cook at all—he was a dropout New York chef…one she'd actually heard of.

She was getting why Larry and his family had gone nuts over the place, but that didn't explain what had happened to her notes. She was sure she taken more of them.

Day Three's notes were definitely not here. Then she remembered…

Raymond Esterling, her Day One breakfast companion.

Who liked the way she listened.

That's what had happened to Day Three.

…and most of Day Four.

Colleen sat down abruptly on the bed in her small cabin.

She ran a hand over the bedspread: Cheyenne weaving done by the owner's wife. She was one of those tall, majestic Native American women that never actually existed in real life. The blanket's geometric reds and golds were as warm as the campfire they'd all sat around while burgers were cooked over open flame on a heavy iron grill earlier this evening—some of the best beef she'd ever tasted.

Whatever in the wide, wide world of Montana was happening to her? A good girl's education in being Japanese hadn't prepared her for this place. Nor a journalist's.

Her ears rang in the silence. No cars at night, no planes. Not even the ocean when she vacationed down at Cannon Beach, Oregon and could pretend the waves were actually the low rumble of I-5 that was never silent in Seattle—easily audible from her apartment on the other side of Lake Union.

A soft whinny drew her back to her feet and out onto the cabin's porch.

Raymond sat astride a big roan—as she'd learned to call his cream-colored mount with dark legs and mane. The sunset lit his gentle face.

He'd "happened" to more than her notes. He was happening to her and none of her training, neither as Kurva Baisotei nor Colleen McMurphy, was ready for it. Not even the city pickup bars had prepared her for him—not even the good ones (if there was such a thing).

Worse, Raymond hadn't resisted her journalistic inquisitiveness.

(*Anta, sensakuzuki,* her sister would curse under her breath—*you are always so nosy,* with the *anta* insult thrown in.)

Raymond hadn't resisted it because she hadn't unleashed it on him. Which was totally unlike her. But he had impressive listening skills as well.

To his credit, after his horseback riding lessons yesterday

and today—in between the lessons he was giving to others— she had a good feel for riding. This afternoon she'd joined a trail ride for beginners and even cantered once; which had been both exhilarating *and* nearly scared her back into the womb.

But she knew so little about him.

He didn't seem to mind talking—he wasn't a reclusive *hikikomori* or even a male jerk "not in touch with his feelings." But it was as if his life beyond the boundaries of the ranch stretched as empty as the scrub prairie.

She knew that was total crap—he was a summer instructor and trail guide, no more. But every time she got ready to pin him down on what he did the other eight months of the year he'd smile at her, adjust her "seat" position, point out an eagle soaring on a thermal, anything to distract her…without appearing to distract her.

Now he sat astride his horse not five feet from the porch of her cabin, looking the quintessential "cowboy in the sunset."

"You can't be some mystic cowboy forever, you know?"

"Evening to you too, Kurva." Somehow he'd gotten that out of her. He also managed to say it like it wasn't a comment on her figure, or rather lack of one, so she let him use it. Instead, he turned her name into a tease, a friendly nickname that didn't chide her for choosing another.

"Evening to you, Raymond. What are you doing up on a horse at this hour?"

"Hoping to take you on an evening ride and see the stars. It's a warm night, but you might want a jacket." Never quite a question, yet not a statement either. As if coaxing her along like a reluctant horse. She didn't appreciate the metaphor but couldn't find the urge to fight it either.

Her own mount, a patient bay named Gumdrop of all silliness, trailed behind him on a lead. Colleen was really getting the vernacular down. She wanted to do a little horse-words rap there on the porch but resisted it. Instead she grabbed a polar fleece off a hook inside the door and climbed up into the saddle.

Seattle girl in the saddle girl
*Astride some rawhide like a way cool—bri—*No!

Her mind nearly strangled itself when her inner rap artist cast up "bride" for worst-rhyming-word-choice-of-the-century award. Definitely not!

The vertiginous Big Sky of Montana expanded even more as they rode up past the cabins and over the rise at a lazy, side-by-side plod. Gumdrop's head bobbed easily, no longer nearly jerking Colleen out of the saddle each time the horse leaned down to crop some grass as they went along.

In the sky, golds found reds.

Reds hinted at impending purples.

Soon Raymond reined to a halt and pointed to the west, "Venus."

Colleen didn't know where to look.

Raymond pulled his mount close beside her so that she could easily follow the line of his pointing arm.

It took her a moment to pick the sparkling point of light out of the red-gold sky, then she had it. It hung above the silhouetted-black mountains like a diamond.

"Planet light, planet bright, First planet I see tonight, I wish I may, I wish I might, Have this wish I wish tonight." Ray's voice was as soft as the call of a passing bird. "Mead-owlark," he filled in for her.

"This seems to be the sort of place that wishes come true." It really was. The pale dry grass lay in golden waves over the rolling prairie. Far below—she didn't realize they'd wandered so far as she had watched the shifting light—lay the cozy cluster of ranch buildings: lodge, barns, and cabins. The next farm over, a big-spread cattle ranch, was just barely visible and looked homey as well.

"What do you wish for, Colleen Baisotei?" He said it right. It was as if he couldn't quite leave her names alone but had to play with them like cat toys. It seemed to make him happy to do so and, curiously, it didn't bother her. Words were her toys as well. She liked that in a man.

"What do I wish for? Not this."

"You don't?"

"Not really. The beauty here is like a drug. Perhaps in small doses, but I'd miss the city too much as well."

"I know," his voice was as soft as the night. "I come here for the summers, retreat to my city in the fall. But I don't think about that now. Now, I am simply here."

"A cowboy."

"They let me play at being one."

Colleen liked that about him, too. He knew what he himself was, even if she didn't know what he was in the real world. And now she understood why. Whereas she— "Huh!"

"What?"

"I'm…not sure what to wish for." Peace with her parents? There was a greater chance of a forest fire in Antarctica. Finding… Colleen didn't know what to plug in there. That bothered her. She really should know.

Sure, she was doing fine. She had good friends in Seattle, whether for a quiet dinner or to go out dancing: square dancing at the Tractor, Britpop Thursday at the Lo-Fi, or bottom-trawling at the J&M. Her job sent her traipsing up and down the Northwest until she knew it like the back of her hand, but kept discovering new things there anyway. Men were pleasant and easy. She knew there was a type of man who looked at her and melted, and she didn't mind that either.   Slim-Japanese-with-dark-hair-well-down-her-back slayed them…another advantage to America over Japan where she was just another potential housewife. Dressing in a tight tube-top at least doubled her yield.

But what to spend an actual wish on…

She turned to him, "What's yours?"

"I would think that was obvious from the moment you walked into the ranch kitchen, Ms. McMurphy."

And when he said it, it was.

She turned from the diamond light of Venus to inspect Raymond Esterling, itinerant horse guide and otherwise unknown. He was what she wasn't. Melting-pot American versus pure-blood Japanese. Sandy blond and fair skinned. Easygoing to her own hyper tendencies—though those seemed to go quiet around him.

"I didn't come here looking to be a summer cowboy fling." Yet he'd grown on her enough over these last days to make it a reasonable consideration.

"Can't say that I've ever been much for flings myself. Every time I try them, I get burned."

"But you're willing to try me? I burn men baaaad! Just warning you."

"I expect, despite my mortal fear of fire, that you are well worth the risk." He also knew how to slay her with a simple piece of flattery. It might be a line, but it was a good one.

"Let's find out."

4

For five more fun-filled days, and five enchantingly rigorous nights, Henderson's Ranch had delivered. She'd fished, learned to cook her trout on a heated rock by a wilderness campfire (though she'd passed on learning how to gut and clean the fish), gone horseback on a wildlife photo safari (she'd bagged a fox, two elk, and a rare bobcat with her camera), and even discovered some skill with a bow and arrow.

She'd also unearthed a bottomless need for how Raymond Esterling could make her feel.

Feel?

Dear gods, it was like she hadn't known the meaning of the word. Her body had responded to his in ways she'd never imagined. His hand on her calf as he checked her stirrup was enough to wrap her entire body in a warm heat. Even now it burned through her memory despite his having left her bed to start his morning chores.

And what she felt inside was equally foreign.

Demanding that her journalistic objectiveness chronicle what was happening to her resulted in—no answers.

Instead, like the splash of cold water that sent her scrabbling for the covers, she was reminded that her idyll was done. This was Last Day, Departure Day.

By this evening she'd be at SeaTac airport, waiting for her best friend Ruth Ann to pick her up and get her good and drunk. Except she didn't feel the need to. Ray had somehow purged her soul of her parents far more than the most exotic cocktail. Going trawling for a bedmate at the J&M, after she'd had a taste of what Ray could make her feel, would be beyond pointless.

Yes, he could make her feel. And by his desperate groans and happy sighs, she knew she did the same in return.

They'd started their final night together with another sunset ride. This time he'd brought a blanket and they'd made love together under the stars. Once before, she'd done it outdoors, fast and desperate on Golden Gardens beach at a college bonfire party, the fear of imminent discovery adding to the hurry.

Last night had been a slow, languid adventure under a brilliant canopy of starlight. When the half moon rose, it had turned the prairie pale yellow and was more than bright enough for them to appreciate each other visually as well as physically. She'd come to like the way Ray looked, a great deal. He was lean but strong. And only six inches taller meant that instead of her face being crushed to a man's chest when they embraced, she could lay her head on his shoulder and nestle against his neck.

She was a journalist because she loved learning new things.

The things Ray had taught her she could place in no article, but they'd been written indelibly upon her skin and emotions.

But now it was time to go. Showered and packed, she was surprised at the hugs she received after breakfast. The women in particular made a point of saying how glad they were to have met her. It felt genuine.

There! That was the hook on her travelogue about this place.

It didn't feel genuine—it *really was* genuine.

She might have become closer to the staff than the tourists, but as they all gathered together for departure, there were many warm farewells.

Colleen stood in the midday-flight time group, waiting for the helicopter to return from the morning-flight group. New arrivals were inbound for their own adventures, welcomed, and were escorted to their freshly cleaned cabins.

Then Ray arrived and cut her out of the herd. She went willingly until they were alone with the horses in the barn.

"Kurva Colleen. May I see you again?"

"Gods, please, yes. But I'll be in Seattle."

"So you said. I'll come looking for you there when I'm done being a cowboy."

"You'd better."

His kiss made that promise as the distant thrum of the helicopter approached to whisk her away.

Dateline, done.

*L*arry loved the piece. For the first time, it passed beneath his evil editor's pen without a single tick-mark or correction. Her next assignment started tomorrow, learning about building boat sails. There were several premier sail lofts in Seattle and she had a very nice contract to write a multi-page marketing-promo article about them for one of the glossy magazines.

But she didn't care about any of that.

She cared about the simple text message, "J&M, 8pm. R"

It would be good to just sit with Ruth Ann, drink a Mai Tai or a Mango Daiquiri, and catch up. She'd been back two weeks. Back? As if time was now measured in distance from Montana.

Out of habit and the lingering Seattle summer heat—rather than thinking about attracting men—she wore a clingy tube-top, short shorts, and sandals, and brushed her hair out long. For once it wasn't about torturing men or even finding one.

She'd already found one, and was discovering that she wasn't getting over him as she'd expected. Her sometimes-cowboy was persevering in her thoughts—like a good story that was hard to forget. Somehow, she couldn't quite remember how, she'd let him slip away without any way to contact him. He was always good at using distraction. Perhaps he hadn't wanted to keep in touch.

Colleen had considered calling the ranch, but he would be gone soon. The short Montana summer was ending. With the start of school, their number of guests would plummet and the extra hands wouldn't be needed. Yet some part of her waited.

She went with the familiar J&M daiquiri for coolness. She also managed to snag her and Ruth Ann's favorite table. It was small, but close by the door. It offered a good view of the male wildlife down the long bar as well as at the small street-side tables outside the windows. A hundred-and-thirty years of drinking had happened here (with a one-year hiccup in '09 that had been devastating until a new owner was found), and she could feel the history every time. It was deep and solid.

The band in the back was just getting rolling. Country-rock tonight. In another hour, conversation would approach the impossible and everyone would move onto the dance floor. For now, shouting was only necessary in the deeper sections of the bar, and the dancers still had room to do some moves.

The parade of men and women through the door barely registered on her. She could see that she was registering on them, but that was the point. Dates were having to poke their men in the ribs, some of them sharply, to keep them moving.

Then one man arrived by himself—which wasn't unusual.

Dressed in typical Seattle: sneakers, jeans, and a UW Huskies t-shirt.

But his gait was odd.

As if he'd just…gotten off a horse.

Ray smiled down at her as he strode up to the table like he was still roaming the prairie.

"You're not 'R'." But he was. Not Ruth Ann. Raymond. She hadn't even looked at the sender on the message.

"You told me you liked this place."

"I do," then she caught herself and patted the seat beside her. "Now I really do."

"And I thought you were dressed that way for me." He sat beside her.

"No, just to torment passing strangers."

"I'm hurt. But it definitely works. You're absolutely killing me."

"What are you…?" His t-shirt registered. "Huskies? You're an alum?"

"Not exactly."

She knew there were adult students, but he didn't act like a student.

He cleared his throat as if preparing to lecture.

He worked there!

"UW Professor Raymond Esterling, specializing in advanced robotics, particularly communication protocols with natural language. That means how robots and people speak to each other."

"You like the way I listen," she recalled the very first thing he'd ever said to her. Of course he would appreciate that.

His nod was easy as he ordered a beer from a passing waitress, as if it was as natural as could be. Of course, she liked the way he communicated too. Except when he evaded her.

"You knew all that time that I was from Seattle and you didn't say anything?" A part of her that had been strangely quiescent over the last two weeks stirred to life. Like one of the Front Range's hibernating bears starting to wake up. She didn't know yet if she was of the angry variety.

"That's a separate part of my life. My days in this life are pretty intense. All indoors, a lot of computer code, with some mechanics and theory stirred in. For three months every year I get to ride horses and look at the horizon."

"And snare willing ranch guests."

"Tally of one so far. But based on that narrow statistical sample, I'd say it was absolutely worth the risk. Don't you agree?"

The last, gentle words were so soft they barely cleared the noise level that the J&M was pumping itself up to.

Raymond Esterling. Robots and horses. He took her hand and the warmth ran up her arm and wrapped around her. Not just her limbs, but that strange place inside where no man had ever belonged.

Belonged.

Something she'd never done. Not in Japan, not really in Seattle. Always a barfly never a...she let the next word come after only briefly shying away. Never a bride.

Yet whether enjoying each other's bodies, riding through the sunset together, or just sitting here knowing they'd be on the dance floor soon, she now knew what the belonging meant.

For outsiders, Henderson's Ranch was about welcome— maybe having a place for a week, or a summer. But with Ray, he made it easy to imagine so much more. There was an absolute rightness that was undeniable.

She leaned in to kiss him. Just before their lips met, she whispered.

"Now I know what to wish for. And yes, absolutely worth it."

IF YOU ENJOYED THIS, YOU MIGHT
ALSO ENJOY:

NATHAN'S BIG SKY (EXCERPT)

A HENDERSON'S RANCH ROMANCE

The silence was deafening.

Nathan gripped the crowbar-handle of his car's jack so tightly that it hurt his hand but he couldn't ease up. It was his sole hope of survival.

The only sound for miles on the emptiness of the Montana prairie was the hot-metal pinging of his cooling Miata sports car, lurched awkwardly to the roadside by a flat tire. The chill of the cold April evening almost hurt his lungs. The sun hadn't quite set; instead it illuminated the clouds of his own breath like some horror movie with a fog machine turned on too high.

How was it that he'd come to this place to die?

Chefs were *not* supposed to die alone in the forsaken wilderness, they were supposed to have a butter-induced heart attack in the middle of a meal service. But the safety of his New York kitchen lay an impossible distance behind him. He'd bolted forty-eight hours ago, sleeping only a few fitful hours in Chicago before punching west as if all the hounds of Hades were after him.

And they'd caught up with him in the form of a monster.

Two days to cross most of the country and now, like a gunslinger fated to his doom, he was going to be murdered in the emptiness of the Montana wilderness by the largest cow ever born.

It put Paul Bunyan's mythically massive blue ox Babe to shame.

Purest black, it was an inkblot on the continuance of Nathan's life.

Horns the length of a New York cabbie's woes sprang from either side of its head, ending in points that looked sharper than his finest boning knife.

He'd hit Choteau, Montana, in the late afternoon for directions, as his little brother's instructions had turned out to be utterly useless: "Henderson Ranch, just west of Choteau." There wasn't a single app on his phone that told him where the ranch might be. There'd also been no answer on his brother's phone, but he was used to that. Apparently most of the ranch was beyond the pale of civilization and didn't have reception. His brother had always been useless about answering the phone anyway, unless you were a pretty girl—them he'd always had a sixth sense for, even on a blocked number.

Maybe Patrick's directions sucked because he was messing with his big brother. Or maybe it was because he assumed Nathan would never cross west of the Hudson River—which historically was a reasonable assumption—so it wasn't worth the effort to be more descriptive.

A Choteau (*Cho-toe* that was almost *Sho-toe*) local had known the name, however. In a town only three blocks long, it made sense that he did. "Just go down the highway apiece until you hit Anderson's farm. Can't miss it. He has the last big white cow barn this side of Augusta. Take a right on the main road and go on until you've just about hit the mountains. Out onto the dirt a ways. That'll set you in the right place."

The "highway" was a narrow two-lane called Montana 287.

By the time Choteau was two miles behind him, he'd passed two Andersons, an Andersen, and an Andreassen. This driveway had no mailbox that he could see, but it had a big white barn and a road along one side of the property. The map on his cell phone said that Augusta was fifty miles ahead. Telling him "the last big barn before Augusta" counted as a local having fun setting up the stranger.. He must have taken one look at Nathan's two-seater Miata and painted a little mental target on Nathan's forehead—just as the monster cow now had one painted on Nathan's life.

The turnoff road was a lane and a half wide. Nathan guessed that in its favor, it was paved and had an actual stop sign where it met the "highway." Sunlight was streaming out the backside of the sign through several bullet holes. He wondered if someone was going to shoot him for being in a sports car instead of a pickup with a gun rack.

Did upstate New York even have roads like this one—not even two lanes wide and with no painted stripes? Or was that only legal west of the Mississippi? Manhattan and Long Island certainly didn't. During his five years in Paris, he'd rarely been farther out than the Metro could carry him.

For thirty miles past the white cow barn, he drove unknow-ingly toward his doom as the mountains drew closer and closer. He kept assuming he'd reach them in another few miles and they insisted on teasing him just like his brother. After the unremit-ting flatness of the Great Plains, they had loomed tall and rough to the west as seen from Choteau. Now he was discovering that Australia wasn't the only place that had an Outback.

The peaks kept growing bigger and climbing higher but

the land remained flatter than the ocean off Coney Island on a hot summer's day. The peaks' jagged flanks were shrouded in snow despite it being April. He turned on the Miata's heater as the sun settled toward the west, but he left the convertible top down because the view was so amazing. The blue sky arced forever over him until the mountains sliced it off like a kid's construction project: sharp, jagged, unreal.

Each time he'd passed a ranch, he checked the name, but none said Henderson. He even pulled out his phone to check that he'd remembered it right—and almost drove his car into the gaping ditch. Not a good idea. For all he knew, there might not be another person down this road for a week. He'd seen a few tractors—which were far bigger than he thought they would be—far out in the fields, but no one else on the road.

With a crash and thud that made him check his rearview to see if he'd left an axle on the road behind him, the pavement ended.

"Out onto the dirt a ways." Maybe the old-timer in Choteau hadn't been completely setting him up..

He slowed down to preserve his suspension. A cloud of brown dust obliterated his past. If he wanted to turn around, he'd have to eat his own dust. That sounded like a properly cowboy-like metaphor for the last decade of his life. Two days ago he'd cut every tie to that past. If only he could figure out how that had led him to the Montanan Outback, he wouldn't feel quite so overwhelmed at the moment. Twenty-eight years old and his life fit in a two-seater sports car—with room to spare. That might not be right, but it didn't make it any less true.

For the last ten miles he'd been hoping to meet someone on the road to ask directions again. Or maybe how to escape, little knowing it would soon be too late.

The dirt road narrowed and then he actually hoped he

didn't meet anyone because he'd have to crawl to the side to get by them. Out here he wasn't threatened by ditches anymore, they'd disappeared along with the pavement, but instead by barbed wire running close down either side of the dirt track. Not a chance that his Soul Red Metallic paint job would survive the encounter.

After a few miles of dodging potholes and gritting his teeth over washboard ripples, he started looking for a place to turn around. The road wasn't wide enough to be sure he could turn even his small car without dinging it up.

He'd been climbing slowly since Choteau, and spring had turned back into winter. There was a bitter snap to the evening air that promised what looked like snow and ice up ahead...really *was* snow and ice up ahead. By this point the mountains were so high they looked as if they were going to roll over and land on him.

Manhattan didn't have places like this. Neither did Paris, where he'd done his time at Le Cordon Bleu and three years servitude for Chef Guevarre—may his brutal training and magnificent palate both be cursed. There was something wrong about the flatness behind and the impossible mountains ahead.

Then, topping a low rise, facing straight into the setting sun, he was confronted by the beast from the underworld that was going to kill him.

He'd slammed on the brakes, skidding sideways on the washboard gravel, and barely managed to avoid hitting the cow. A tire caught in a pothole where it had blown with a loud bang that scared him almost as much as the creature of his doom had.

Now he stood in the middle of the road between his crippled car, pinging the last dying notes of its hot-metal song, and the monstrous black cow that was about to charge him.

The thing didn't so much as blink its malevolent eyes, as if it was trying to hypnotize him.

His only weapon choices were his chef's knives, which would be very useful if the cow was already dead and butchered but not until then, and his car's jack handle. Retreating into his car and pulling up the convertible's roof would be pointless—this monster was so big it could practically step over the Miata. And the tips of its horns were actually wider than the car itself.

His ears rang with the silence, now broken only by a scuffing of one New York metro bus-sized hoof as the cow prepared to charge. Nathan had served a thousand roasts, ten thousand steaks, and this meal-still-on-the-hoof knew it. It had come to exact revenge for all of its spiritual forebears... fore-steaks?

The last thing Nathan was going to smell was the crackling dry grass of the prairie, the biting chill of the fast-approaching night, and the hot breath of the demon cow so big it seemed to block out even the vast expanse of the Montana sky. There had been fourteen hundred miles of flat since Chicago, but here, with his back up against the mountains, the vast horizon seemed far bigger than should be possible. His last-ever vision would be to actually see the curvature of the earth.

Then, impossibly, as if it wasn't bad enough that his epitaph was going to read: *Here a once-decent chef was trampled to death by a cow*—trampled sounded like a marginally more pleasant way to go than gored—he heard a clip-clop sound coming from behind him.

He didn't dare turn, because he knew the beast-cow would charge the moment he looked aside.

Still, the sound behind him grew.

Unable to stand it any longer—the sound was so close—

he spun and raised his foot-long jack handle in one last desperate bid for life.

Backed by the sun, a silhouetted cowboy sat up on a horse even taller than the cow and looked down at Nathan from under the brim of his cowboy hat.

"What are you doing out in the road?"

Not cowboy, cowgirl. A soft voice, but no less disgusted for all that. Against the dazzling sun he could see that she wore cowboy boots, a heavy leather jacket, and had a rifle tucked close to hand.

Hope?

Maybe she could shoot the demon cow before it trampled, trompled, gored, or whatever demon cows did.

He tried to speak, but his throat was clogged dry with fear and road dust. The air was so dry it seemed to suck the moisture right out of him.

She rode around him and his car as if he wasn't even there. "Go on now, Lucy. Scoot!"

A demon beast named Lucy?

He'd had a great Aunt Lucy, but she hadn't been very fierce—more the quiet and retiring type, which was perhaps inevitable beside her husband's garrulous stockbroker charisma.

The woman rode her black-and-white patterned horse up to the "monster cow from the underworld" before he could warn her off.

Yet, in a startlingly sudden surrender, the gigantic animal turned and ambled back through a broken gap in the barbed wire fence that Nathan hadn't noticed. As it walked, he recognized the scuffing sound that he'd thought proceeded a deadly charge—it was just the sound the cow made by walking.

After riding her horse through the gap as well, she then swung a long leg over the back of the saddle and came down out of the sky. Paying no more attention to him than if he was a bump in the road, she pulled out some tools and walked up to the fence.

He could only watch—numb with his unexpected last-second stay of execution and the biting cold—as she repaired the fence. It was only the work of minutes before she had three fine strands of barbed wire strung back up between the posts; her and the cow on one side and he and his broken car on the other. The flimsy wires had no chance of stopping a baby cow, never mind the demon cow Lucy, currently tearing at the low dead grass.

The woman had been towering in the saddle; on the ground she was still tall. Perhaps slender beneath the heavy leather jacket. Straight, light blond hair fell past her shoulders. Her cheeks were rosy with the cold, which he'd always thought was just a saying.

When she finished, he finally found his voice before she could disappear back into the landscape as eerily as she'd arrived.

"Excuse me, can you tell me how to get to Henderson Ranch?"

"I can," he could just see her eyes beneath the wide brim of her cowboy hat. They were as brilliant blue as the sky and seemed to be laughing at him, though her mouth wasn't. What was it with locals today?

"Would you mind telling me?"

"Not a bit," and she let it hang long enough to make him sigh.

The failing sun caught the cloud of his breath in the chill air.

"You're standing on Henderson land."

"I am?" he looked down at the road, but it was keeping its secrets to itself. "This doesn't look like a ranch, it looks like a whole bunch of nothing."

"It's two *ranches*," she sounded miffed by his description, which, he decided on review, hadn't been the most tactful thing he'd ever said. "You're standing on Henderson's, but your passenger seat is on mine—property line runs up the middle of the lane. You've been on Mac and Ama's land for the last five miles or so. If you'd like, I can chop your car in two and then you'll be off *my* family's land."

"That's okay. I like my car the way it is."

"Even with the flat?"

"Okay, except for the flat." Was this what passed for a sense of humor out here, or was she about to pull the rifle hanging on her horse's saddle and make good on her offer— maybe shooting his poor car for trespassing before skinning it? Perhaps it would be safer if he kept her talking. "What are you doing way out here?"

"Riding the fence."

He assumed that meant something to someone other than him, but he couldn't figure out how to ask what. Her horse stepped up to her and rested its chin over her shoulder. She reached up a gloved hand and patted it on the cheek a couple of times.

"I was looking for different," and it didn't get more different than the woman in front of him.

"Thought you were looking for Henderson's."

"I was. I am," and he was on the verge of being turned into a babbling idiot. He'd left New York looking for a change. For something he'd never done, someone he'd never been. Couldn't get more different than a burned-out New York chef and a tall, blond cowgirl out "riding a fence" who had a horse for a pet.

"Their drive is another mile yet, on the left. Can't miss it," she tipped her head toward farther down the road. Then, in a move so smooth she might have been doing it since birth, she stepped one foot up into a high stirrup and swung atop the tall horse. He'd briefly dated an American Ballet Theater dancer—sleeping through her performance had not earned him many bonus points—who didn't have the grace or posture of this cowgirl. Cow-woman. Was that a real phrase? She stepped once more into line with the low sun and he lost her in the glare.

"Thanks," he called out. One of his more charming lines.

"Need help with the tire?"

"I can change a flat."

Her blinding silhouette nodded as if that might be a miracle worth witnessing, then tipped her hat and turned to ride away. He couldn't argue with that conclusion, but it would be too embarrassing to admit his gross incompetence.

"Will I see you again?"

"It depends," she spoke over her shoulder without fully turning.

"On what?" Nathan had to call more loudly as she headed away perpendicular to the road.

"On how long I can avoid you."

UNWILLING TO TURN, Julie Larson kept an ear out. It took a bit, but then she heard a soft laugh.

A minute later, the rattling sound of someone jacking a car—a sound far enough away to be no louder than the ticking of a lone cricket. Anything else was lost beneath the sound of the last of the dry winter grass swishing against Clarence's hocks, but that laugh intrigued her. She didn't know why the man made her more prickly than a stinging nettle.

This had been the last stretch of the fence line. There were a half dozen places where the winter had snapped a post and occasional runs where wood rot had finally taken down a whole stretch of wire, but nothing bad in the entire run. In the morning she'd grab one of the hands and a truck; they'd have the spring pasture put together before the cattle were ready for it. Old Lucy had somehow slipped in early, but she'd been a certified escape artist since her third day afoot.

Will I see you again?

"Not a chance, city boy. I've already got my big strong man. Don't I?" she leaned forward to scrub at the side of Clarence's neck as his ears pricked back to listen to her. What was it with city boys and a woman on a horse? For that matter, what was it with cowboys and a woman on a horse?

Number One question: *You aren't married?* (delivered with an astonished gasp). Twenty-six and single was definitely a crime. Or at least a freak of nature.

Number Two question: *Wa'll how about me, darlin'?* (as if a lame Texas accent worked wonders in the Montana Front Range).

I was looking for different.

What had he meant by that? Didn't matter—he was Mac and Ama's problem now.

She leaned in just enough for Clarence to lift up to a quick trot. It was still comfortably above freezing, but there wasn't a cloud in sight so it would chill down fast once the sun hit the horizon. Even now the long shadows of Old Baldy and Rocky Mountain stretched across the prairie leaving her in a narrow slash of red-gold sunlight across the still-brown prairie.

Julie resisted Clarence's urge to gallop. She didn't want him to get all heated before a cold night in the barn.

Different. The city boy had that right. A sports car in the land of pickup trucks. A convertible in a place where rocketing winds and plunging temperatures defined seven months of the year. He had tousled dark hair, warm eyes, and an easy smile that seemed to be aimed first of all at himself.

Different. She looked at the sweep of land around her, the Larson barn, house, and sheds coming into view, and wondered at it. There were so many things to love here, but different wasn't one of them.

Clarence asked again with a shift in his stride. She eased off and let him slip into a canter. Even big, handsome boys like him deserved to have some fun. She tugged down on the brim of her hat to make sure she didn't lose it and decided that she deserved some fun, too. She gave Clarence his head and between one stride and the next he took her to the pure exhilaration of a full gallop over the rolling pastureland.

Why anyone would want *different* when they could have this, she didn't know.

Available at fine retailers everywhere:
HENDERSON'S RANCH

M.L. Buchman started the first of, what is now over 50 novels and as many short stories, while flying from South Korea to ride his bicycle across the Australian Outback. Part of a solo around the world trip that ultimately launched his writing career.

All three of his military romantic suspense series—The Night Stalkers, Firehawks, and Delta Force—have had a title named "Top 10 Romance of the Year" by the American Library Association's *Booklist*. NPR and Barnes & Noble have named other titles "Top 5 Romance of the Year." In 2016 he was a finalist for Romance Writers of America prestigious RITA award. He also writes: contemporary romance, thrillers, and fantasy.

Past lives include: years as a project manager, rebuilding and single-handing a fifty-foot sailboat, both flying and jumping out of airplanes, and he has designed and built two houses. He is now making his living as a full-time writer on the Oregon Coast with his beloved wife and is constantly amazed at what you can do with a degree in Geophysics. You may keep up with his writing and receive a free starter e-library by subscribing to his newsletter at: www.mlbuchman.com

Join the conversation:
www.mlbuchman.com

Other works by M. L. Buchman: